To misunderstood teachers
and
their misunderstood students
—PB

My Teacher Is a **MONSTER!**

No, I Am Not.

Peter Brown

Little, Brown and Company
New York Boston

Bobby had a big problem at school.
Her name was Ms. Kirby.

Ms. Kirby stomped.

Ms. Kirby roared.

Ms. Kirby was a monster.

Bobby spent his free time in the park,
trying to forget his teacher problems.

But one Saturday morning, on the way to his favorite spot, Bobby found a terrible surprise.

Bobby wanted to run!
He wanted to hide!
But he knew that would
only make things worse.

Robert, you don't need to raise your hand out here.

What were you going to say?

I was going to say, "Hello, Ms. Kirby."

Hello, Robert.

There was an awkward silence.
And then a gust of wind changed everything.

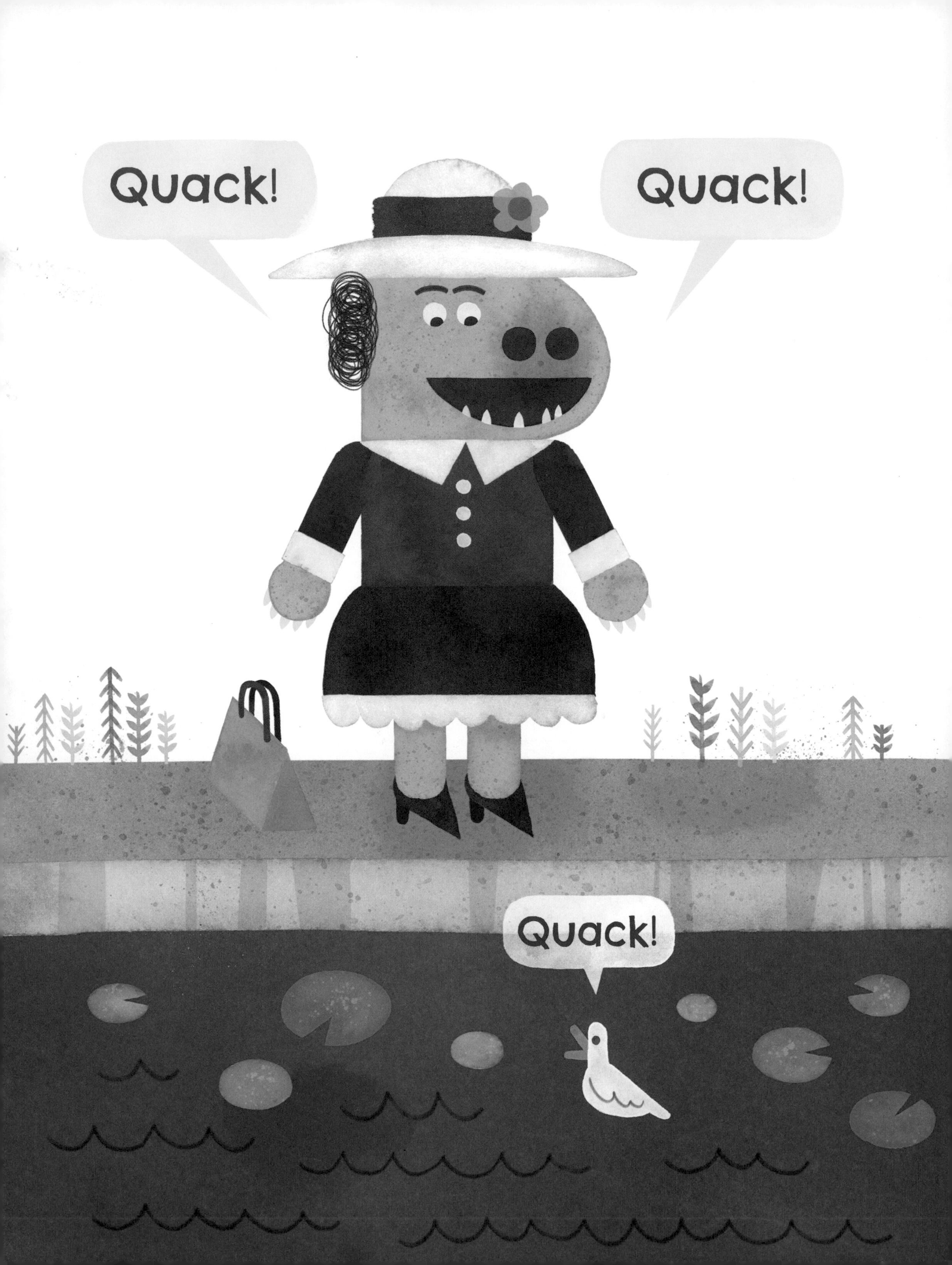
Quack!
Quack!
Quack!

When they were all quacked
out, Bobby had an idea.

You should see my
favorite spot in the park.

Bobby tossed his paper
airplane into the sky

and it flew

and it flew

and it flew.

By lunchtime, Bobby and Ms. Kirby were
happy they had bumped into each other.

But they were ready to say good-bye.

Back at school, Ms. Kirby still stomped.

Ms. Kirby still roared.

But was Ms. Kirby still a monster?

The End

About This Book

The illustrations for this book were made with India ink, watercolor, gouache, and pencil on paper, then digitally composited and colored.

This book was edited by Alvina Ling and designed by Patti Ann Harris and Peter Brown. The production was supervised by Erika Schwartz, and the production editor was Barbara Bakowski.

This book was printed on 140 gsm Gold Sun Woodfree paper. The text was set in Archer, and the display type is Chelsea Market Pro.